Ullans 16

Ullans

THE MAGAZINE FOR ULSTER-SCOTS

Nummer 16, Hairst 2023

Edited by Anne Smyth

ULLANS PRESS

COLLOGUE O ULLANS

Compluthert fur tae gie a heft til tha Ulstèr-Scotch Leid in wor ain hamely tongue an litèrarie scrievins fae tha Lallans o Ulstèr. ULLANS is published by the Ulster-Scots Language Society

The Ulster-Scots Language Society was formed to encourage an interest in traditional Ulster-Scots literature; to promote creative writing in modern Ulster-Scots; to support the use of Ulster-Scots speech and writing in present-day education; and to encourage the Ulster-Scots tradition in music, dance, song, ballads and story-telling. In short, our aim is to promote the status of Ulster-Scots as a traditional language, and to re-establish its dignity as a European regional language with an important part to play in our cultural heritage.

ISBN 978-1-905281-35-0

Front cover: 'Tha Oul Precentor's Hoose', Ballyhemlin, by Philip Robinson.

Contents

Editorial

Just as we were gathering together data for *Ullans 16*, we found ourselves, in common with the rest of the world, in the throes of the Covid pandemic. Reams have been written about its considerable impact on everyone's mental and physical health, and rather than add to them, this issue of the first and best Ulster-Scots journal is about giving you some Ulster-Scots distraction (and maybe inspiration to write a bit yourself!).

Unfortunately, the hiatus in activity caused by Covid also massively delayed the publication of tributes to three huge personalities who in their various ways were of pivotal importance in the work of the Ulster-Scots Language Society over the years and who passed away during the period since our last issue. Although there is a certain diffidence about including them after such a lapse of time, the Society's committee felt it was important to record our appreciation of the contribution these three individuals made, and so tributes to Professor Michael Montgomery, James Fenton and Dr Ian Adamson can be found elsewhere in this issue.

Another article in this issue, this time concerning the restoration of the Ballyhemlin Precentor's Hoose, is a timely reminder of the two highly successful evenings of Ulster-Scots psalms and readings, hosted at the church on 21 September 2018 and 15 November 2019, which were greatly enjoyed by all who attended. We are working towards another such event in the not too distant future, and will get in touch with our membership when arrangements are finalised.

What were we doing during the pandemic? Well, the Society prepared an application for a Covid Resilience Grant from the Ulster-Scots Agency, but the application was unsuccessful because apparently the scheme was focused on the creation of digital resources and our application was 'not a good fit'. We are currently exploring other ways of bringing the writings of Samuel Walker to the publication stage.

April 2019 saw the Language Society raise objections to the content of a book published by Irish Pages with public funding, and the publisher's failure to obtain copyright permissions. There is more about this in the tribute to James Fenton.

That October, Ballywalter Festival featured an R L Moore workshop led by Society officers Philip Robinson and Anne Smyth. The rediscovery of Dr Moore's work on the County Down Ulster-Scots of the 1918 to 1942 period filled a gap in the historical record and was followed by the publication in 2020 under the Ulster-Scots Academy imprint of three books of Moore's research and writing (edited variously by Robinson and Smyth), *The Leevin Tongue: An historical record of Ulster-Scots as a living language in County Down*, and the following year, *The Mystery of Strangford Lough: A Tale of Killinchy and the Ards* and *Wullie Gunyun's Crack frae Clabber Raw*.

Philip Saunders, another Society committee member, has been involved in having the *Fower Gospels* Bible translation made accessible through an Ulster-Scots Bible app. The

Society owes Philip and Heather a great debt of gratitude for heading the translation teams and promoting the translated gospels with enormous enthusiasm.

During Covid and immediately afterwards, a range of additional material was published by Ulster-Scots Academy Press and Ullans Press, and this included both historical writings such as two more May Crommelin books and County Down titles by Mrs J H Riddell, and the work of current writers, such as Steve Dornan (see Al Miller's review elsewhere in this journal) and Fiona McDonald (*Frae Cowie's Craig*). A long-felt need for guidance for new writers was fulfilled by the publication of Philip Robinson's *Ulster-Scots Writers' Guide*, and the same year (2021) saw Philip's *Ulster-Scots Names for Birds* and *Ulster-Scots Names for People: Surnames, First Names, Nicknames and Descriptive Names* appear in print.

Unfortunately, the Society has also felt the need to respond to various manifestations of political and civil service insensitivity and incomprehension, which involved a response in June 2021 to proposals for a 'central translation hub' under the aegis of the Department for Communities, apparently in total disregard for the scarcity of skilled and properly trained translators for Ulster-Scots and for the marked reluctance on the part of government departments to actually commission translations into the language. As so often seems to be the case in the sector, the powers that be have prepared the icing for the cake without even having baked the cake!

A 15-page detailed response from the USLS was also compiled following the release of the report of the Panel of Experts tasked with considering the implementation of the 'New Decade, New Approach' agreement of January 2020. The impetus for this agreement was of course driven by the political need to justify capitulation to politically-motivated demands for an Irish Language Act, and therefore did not prioritise the actual, as opposed to imagined, needs of the Ulster-Scots language. Every one of the 'experts' on the panel was dependent on the Ulster-Scots sector for their employment.

Now the next phase of this process is being progressed by a 'Co-Design Group', the members of which do not appear to have had any previous experience of language planning.

Early in 2021, the Language Society also compiled a response to the Interim UK Evaluation of the European Commission for Regional or Minority Languages.

The Society has also readily facilitated assistance with

Ulster-Scots language matters following requests from other sources. Examples were the briefing for Robbie Meredith of the BBC on National Minority Status prepared in July 2021, and assistance for one of our own members with the production of an educational video based on several Ulster-Scots poems from a range of geographical locations and across the historical continuum.

Possibly one of the most far-reaching changes we have seen is Belfast City Council's decision to permit translation into one language other than English of the name of any street if only 15% of its residents request it. Furthermore, the council reserves to itself the right to authorise the addition of the non-English name regardless of the actual number of residents requesting it. Without expressing a political view (which itself is difficult when commenting on a polit-ically-motivated change in the rules), the Society is deeply concerned about the divisiveness of this policy. Across the Ulster-Scots sector, the word we most often hear used of Ulster-Scots experience of interaction with any public bodies is 'marginalisation'. Belfast City Council has exacerbated this by ruling that only two languages are permissible in the signage, whereas it has always been the Society's position that if any language other than English is introduced then

Ulster-Scots must also be included, or a substantial element of Northern Ireland society – those who identify as Ulster-Scots – is thereby marginalised.

Other reasons, such as cost, for opposing the move have been stated in various media and we do not need to rehearse them here. Queen's University is the Belfast City Council 'approved translator' for all languages. The Council's committee reports usually refer to translations being 'authenticated' by QUB. This apparently means that the applicant can provide a translation and it is then forwarded to Queen's for 'authentication'. Ulster-Scots speakers do not tend to be interested in the weaponising of their language. However, at the request of a member we have provided Ulster-Scots translations of a number of street names in North Belfast.

As will be obvious from the above, the Society has remained active in unobtrusive ways through lockdown and its aftermath. However, its committee has returned to meeting regularly and is reviewing its future programme. We are intending to create a way of keeping in touch with members so that you can be informed about events and projects between issues of *Ullans*, just as in the early days of the Society *Kintra Sennicht* was sent out to the membership. Ideally, we would like to optimise the number of email addresses in our records so that this can have the best possible circulation. This is therefore an appeal to members to please provide us with your email address if you have not already done so. Indeed, we'd like to hear more from you generally, so if you have any views or suggestions (or importantly, submissions for the next issue of *Ullans*) please get in touch.

We hope you enjoy reading this issue – there is plenty in it to take your mind off Covid!

The Ulster-Scots Language Society's greatly esteemed Honorary Vice-President, Will McAvoy (on the right), on the occasion of his 100th birthday on 10th May 2023. Also pictured are (left) Will Cromie and (centre) Charlie Gillen.

Will with his eye on the cake!

Bab M'Keen's Ballymena Sewerage Scheme

Am no' guid at public speakin', bein' o' a backward turn, an' on this accoont I cood na get up like ither great oraters on the late occasions tae speak oot my min' on a subject that at the present time lucks tae be only second in importance tae the Sewez Canal; I mean the sewerage o' Bellamena, an' the watherin' o' Bellamena. A guid deal has been said aboot the former, but it remains for me to produce a skame that 'll dae baith at the same time. It's in the cloods o' the nicht, or the quateness o' the sma' oors o' the mornin' that half o' the great inventions o' modhern days has seen the licht, for it's at these times that men o' thocht, whun the weans hae been in bed an' 'oor or twa, an' the hoose in peace an' quateness, tuck tae the black airt an' ither ill farrant skames, tae search oot the mistheries o' nathur. An' the big clock at the Toon Hall was jest clappin' twa the ither mornin' as I was waukened oot o' my sleep wi' twa thumps on my shouther, an' luckin' up, wha daes I see afore me, an' abune me but my auld acquuantance Airmed Science, the white woman o' the Park. Tae say that I was astonished wad be tae mak' a simple observation, for tae tell the truth I was perfectly dumfoundthered. "In the name o' the Archypellygo (for I thocht it as weel tae gie hir a stomicker) what brings ye here," quo' I, "at this time o' nicht."

"Wheesht," quo' she, "wheesht," an she hel' up yin o' hir freestane fingers, "wheesht, or ye'll wauken Nancy."

"Oh," quo' I, "am gled this nicht she's oot o' the hoose, for she went aff a bit yistherday, an wunna be hame for twa or three days yit. Had she got sicht o' ye here she wad hae grun' ye intil poother tae whiten the heartstane wi'."

"Dae ye think sae, Bab?" quo she. "What wad ye think if she coodna catch me?" an' wi' that she vanished, but kep' taukin' a' the time.

"Bab," quo' she, "whun am stuck up in the Park am a lump o' clye, but whun I tak' tae the country on the ramble, am a spirit, jest a wauf o' wun," an' wi' that she appeared again.

"Weel," quo I, "ye ca'd at an akward time for there's no a drap in the hoose tae weet yer lips wi'."

"Oh, Bab," quo' she, "niver min' that; am quat. I had tae gie it up. Am saftenenin' o' the brain, ye ken."

"By my word, then," quo' I, "if the licker had that effect

o' saftenin' your brain, I dinna ken what it wad dae wi' flesh an' bluid. But what dae ye want wi' me?" quo' I.

"I want," quo' she, "tae meet me an 'oor frae noo at the fower corners, an' then I'll show ye a sicht that if ye hae the wut tae tak' advantage o' it yer fortune's made for iver."

"Aye," quo I, "the auld story, leeve auld horse an' you'll get gress. But I'll gang come what may," an' wi' that she left me.

Weel, at the appointed time I was on the spot, an' there was my rare lass waitin' on me, an' without ony mair adae she passed hir han' ower my een, an' a glammer fell ower them, an' a hole appeared at my feet.

"Whaur am I?" quo I. "I'll gie ye a shillin' if ye tell me whaur I am."

"Yer in the Bellamena o' the future," quo' she, "an' before ye, ye see yin o' the greatest triumphs o' science, past, present or tae come."

"I see naethin but a big hole," quo' I.

"Go forrit tae the edge," quo' she, "an' luck ower," an' a lucked in, an' awa' doon, doon iver sae far went the big hole, an' at the en o' it was clear day licht, an' I thocht I sa' a man luckin' up frae the ither side. I luckt closer, an' may I niver but there was my brither Jamie that went awa' tae

New Azealand fower an' twunty year ago, an' the last word we heerd frae him he was hirdin' sheep amang the scroggery.

"Is that you Jamie ?" quo' I.

"It is Bab," quo' he, "hoo's my da?"

"Oh deed he's richtly," quo' I , "but tell me Jamie, whun did ye come hame?"

"Hame !" quo' he, "am no' at hame ava; am aye in New Azealand."

"Weel, bliss me, what's this onywye ?" quo' I, an I turned roon tae see Airmed Science for an explanation.

"That," quo' she, "is the Gran' Bore Shorage Skame, an' it'll be in use in Bellamena in the year 1948. It was discovered by a fluke, but so great are its advantages that a' toons maun hae it. Ye ken, in the year 1879 the Toon Commissioners commenced a new skame o' what they ca'd the big drains, an' Bellamena grew till fower times the size, an' returned a member o' Parlymint; but up tae 1930 they niver had a wather supply. At that time, efther a big drouth, and the half o' the toon bein' burned twa or three times, the Corportation thocht o' introducin' a wather skame, an' it was decided as there was nae wather on the face o' the earth nearer than Lough Neagh an' it bein' the only ootlet for the big drains in Bellamena, the wathers had become polluted tae sich an extent that the fishermen had threatened the Toon Cooncil wi' John Rea for killin' a' the pullans in the lough. Weel, the Cooncil in its wisdom thocht that what wa'd kill a pullan coodna be guid for folk, an' efther a lang debate resolved tae brek up the fountains o' the great deep by the new skame. Operations were then commenced. There was diggin', an' blastin', an' borin'. They went doon through iron-stane, free-stane, lime-stane, an' whun-stane ; but it was tae nae purpose. There was nae wather tae be had. By this time porther had ris tae half-a-croon a bottle, an' the folk was jest deein' in dizens. Weel, at lang an' last, the borin' brigade wur hemmerin' awa', an' afore they kent whaur they wur, they had brauk through the scroof o' the earth, on the ither side o' the worl', an' come oot on dry lan' in New Azealand."

"Weans, oh!" quo' I, "did ye iver hear the like o' it ? I suppose in the dark they coodna fin' oot whaur they wur gaun, an' sae in place o' hittin' the wathery airt they made a mistak' an' come oot on dry lan'."

"Jest sae," quo' she, "an' the suction o' the hole was sae great at the furst that it drew a' the machinery an' twa o' the Toon Councillors through in wae yin rattle. Weel", quo' she, "tae mak' a lang story short, the people was demented, an' didna ken what tae dae, whun a very cliver engineerer that had made a heap o' nerrow gage railways, made up a new skame tae rin the shorage o' the toon intil the big hole, an' in this wye the toon was cleaned tae perfection, an sae powerful was the suckage o' that hole, that the wather o' Lough Neagh — noo relieved o' the filthy dirt — came gushin' up the pipes, an' intil the hooses, an' frae that there was nae want o' wather in Bellamena, an' the Toon Cooncil had an' oot-let for iver, an' by this means the toon was wathered an' shored at the same time."

As shen as she had daen, I leaned forrit again tae luck doon the hole tae ha'e anither chat wi' my brither an' cries —

"Jamie! Jamie!" as lood as iver I cud, an' wi' that I hears Nancy cryin' —

"Guid bless me, Bab! what's wrang wi' ye"

"Whaur im I," quo' I.

"Ye're in yer ain hoose," quo' she; an' for the last 'oor ye ha'e been dosin' in the corner there, an' mutterin' tae yersel ivery five minutes — jest sae, an' weel, weel. If it hadna been that I kent ye wur sober I wud hae said ye wur drunk."

"An' is it a dhrame?" quo' I, " an' did I no' see the Gran' Bore Shorage Skame, an' my brither Jamie at the yin en' an' me at the ither?" an I begun an' toul Nancy the hale thing, keepin' the big woman in the back grun'.

"Bab," quo' she, "its afore something, an I wud advise ye tae tell Mesther Tamson whun ye see him gaun tae skool in the mornin'."

Weel, I speered at the mesther, an' he luckt ower the jogaffa, menshurashun, an' the "rule o' three," but cud mak' naethin' o' it; an' jest whun we wur in the middle o' saerchin' Nancy comes in wi' a leap an quo' she — "Didn't a tell ye, it was afore somethin'!"

"What was it," quo' I, jest brustin' tae hear.

"The wee sprickled hen has laid a dooble-yoked egg!" quo' she, "an' that's what it was afore."

"Ye're an auld gommey," quo' I, "an' has jest as much wut as the sprickled hen," an' I left hir an' the mesther in clean disgust. Weemen hae nae wut onywye.

BAB M'KEEN.

The Old Precentor's House at Ballyhemlin Non-Subscribing Presbyterian Church

Ballyhemlin Non-Subscribing Presbyterian Church

The Ballyhemlin congregation dates its beginning from a sermon delivered to a large audience in a field at Kircubbin by the Rev. Dr Montgomery in the spring of 1833. Mrs Allen, an original member of the congregation, recalled the sermon in the field at Nunsquarter:

"It was a very warm day and he preached the greater part of the evening and all the countryside was there. At the conclusion of the service he sat down exhausted and covered his head with a large orange coloured handkerchief."

This was followed by a number of services held in a barn loft in Ballyhalbert. A number of families from the villages of Kirkcubbin, Ballyhalbert and Ballywalter then sent a memorial to the Remonstrant Synod of Ulster praying that they might be formed into a congregation to be called Ballyhemlin. The synod consented and a meeting house was then built on land donated by the Allen Family, equidistant from the three villages in the middle of the peninsula.

Presbyterians, Psalm-singing and Precentors

A PRECENTOR WANTED, BY THE RE-MONSTRANT Congregation of Ballyhemlin. Salary, 8*l.* per annum, with a good Dwelling-House rent free.
Apply to the Rev. ALEXANDER ORR, Kirkcubbin.

In those days the worship in the meeting house – as in all Presbyterian churches in Ireland and Scotland – involved the singing of the Biblical Psalms only, on the grounds that it was proper to sing in public worship words that had been written for that purpose in scripture.

This tradition of 'exclusive Psalmody' (that is, no hymns) also meant no instrumental accompaniment, and it required the congregational singing to be led by a Singing Clerk or Precentor. Before that, psalms were the only musical component of public worship in Presbyterian churches. The strict view that only Psalms should be used in worship was further reinforced by the view that the actual words of the psalms should be used only in sabbath services and should not be used in singing practices for the purpose of learning the tunes.

The precentor, then, had the job of teaching the congregation to sing the psalms. It should be noted that at this time all singing was unaccompanied by an organ.

A Precentor in those days did a number of jobs. As well as leading the singing in worship, he taught 'singing classes' for the tunes and harmonies in the Scottish Psalter. He also usually was a school teacher and also the clerk of session for the congregation.

[Opposite: Display panels on the Old Precentor's House.]

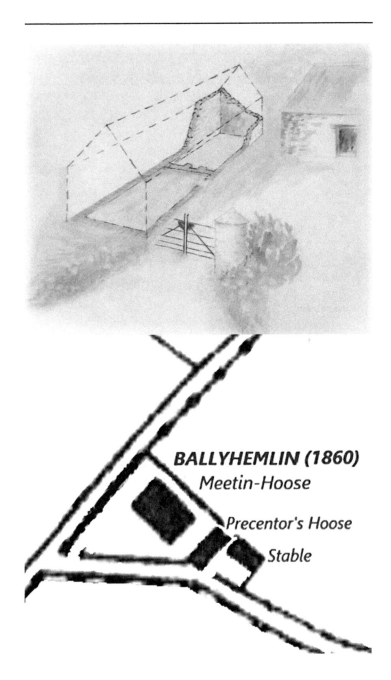

BALLYHEMLIN (1860)
Meetin-Hoose

Precentor's Hoose

Stable

Tha Oul Precentor's Hoose at Ballyhemlin

Soon after Ballyhemlin opened in 1834, it was found almost impossible to obtain the services of a regular Precentor and 'Singing Master' as the nearest village was several miles away. Other Presbyterian churches, even in rural locations, had a school nearby, making it convenient for the Precentor to double up as the local schoolmaster.

The response to this problem at Ballyhemlin was to build a rent-free house for any suitable Precentor who would accept the position, in addition to an annual salary of £8. It was a novel solution, and the Ballyhemlin Precentor's House is possibly unique as the only purpose-built Precentor's dwelling ever built in Ireland. It was a small, two-roomed cottage built about 1840 with stone walls and a slated roof.

When instrumental music in the form of a harmonium and hymn-books (to replace the Psalter) were introduced to the Ballyhemlin church in the 1870s, the days of Psalm-singing and Precentors came to an end, and the dwelling-house was given over to accommodate a caretaker. From this time the 'Sexton's House', as it became known, wasn't considered anything special and in the early 1900s other small outbuildings were added to the old stable.

The Restoration

The *Oul Precentor's Hoose* was partially demolished in the 1970s to allow for a new church entrance and car park, leaving the ruined remains under a heap of stones. Over the years, weeds, grass, ivy and wild flowers took hold and covered the pile of stones until, one day in 2020, some of the ivy was pulled back and a stone wall was revealed, still intact. It was in fact the corner of the Precentor's house. The pile of stones was then carefully removed to uncover the outline and lower part of the gable end of the house. Further excavations brought to light the original floor of that half of the house. Research then showed that a series of advertisements had been placed in local newspapers searching for a Precentor for Ballyhemlin, and by 1843 and 1846 the inducements included "a good Dwelling-House rent free".

The project to restore this important part of Presbyterian history – the first Precentor's House in Ireland – and to provide interpretation panels in the Ulster-Scots language was undertaken by a working group of the Ulster-Scots Academy that included Billy Carlile, Philip Robinson, Paddy McAvoy and Derek Rowlinson, working closely in partnership with Rev. Ian Gilpin and the congregation of Ballyhemlin Non-Subscribing Presbyterian Church.

Philip Robinson took on the bulk of the physical la-
bour, but his pre-retirement experience of the reconstruc-
tion of exhibit buildings in the Ulster Folk and Transport
Museum and past membership of the Northern Ireland
Historic Buildings Council were invaluable in providing a

sympathetic approach to the restoration of this fascinating part of the heritage of the Ards Peninsula. The project has also resulted in the production of the only solely Ulster-Scots language signage in Northern Ireland. It has shown what can be done with a minimum of expense, the right personnel – and above all, a commitment to authenticity.

Billy Carlile

The story of 'The Wild Deer', 'Cloughey Shore' and other poems

Philip Robinson

The 1883 Shipwreck of the *Wild Deer* on the North Rock, Cloughey

The Wild Deer: Pictured here in New Zealand in 1872, "The Wild Deer" was an emigrant ship on its eleventh voyage to New Zealand when it set sail with 209 passengers from Glasgow on the 9th of January 1883. In a fearful storm near midnight, the ship broke up on the North

Rock, about two miles off the Cloughey shore on the Ards
Peninsula. All passengers and crew were saved, mostly rescued by the heroic efforts of men from the nearby fishing
village of Portavogie.

Before the days of harbour-based trawlers, the Portavogie
fishermen used small flat-bottomed fishing boats called
'pincks' that were kept 'beached' on the shore. On the
night of the shipwreck, these men were raised by their local Presbyterian minister, Rev. Alexander W. Whitley, and
repeatedly braved the storm by rowing out in their small
fishing boats until all 209 were safely shuttled to the shore
where they were given shelter in Cloughey church and local
homes.

The Otago Scots settlement in New Zealand: The destination for the passengers of the *Wild Deer* was the province of Otago in New Zealand, which had been purchased by the Free Church of Scotland for a new Scots colony, with its principal town as Dunedin (New Edinburgh). A Scottish settlement in New Zealand had first been mooted in 1842 by Scottish architect and politician George Rennie, who hoped to establish 'a new Edinburgh' in the southern hemisphere. Dunedin became a feasible project once the New Zealand Company purchased the large Otago block from Ngāi Tahu in 1844.

Divisions within the Church of Scotland transformed Rennie's original plan. Unhappy with patronage and state control, 400 clergy and about one-third of lay people quit the established church. Some of these dissenters, including Rev. Thomas Burns who became the settlement's first minister, saw Otago as a home for a new 'Free Church'. Two-thirds of the original Otago settlers were Free Church Presbyterians.

Knox Presbyterian Church, Dunedin: Besides about a dozen 'single young ladies' from Ulster on board the *Wild Deer* who had been sponsored by the educationalist Vere Foster in Belfast, there was a 71-year-old businessman from Ballymena. George Tombe had sold his shop in Ballymena

KNOX PRESBYTERIAN CHURCH.

to join the new colony just before the *Wild Deer*'s final voyage. His funeral was from this church in 1887 and his obituary noted that he was a dedicated and active church member but often unable to attend meetings because of leg injuries he had received in the shipwreck. George Tombe, like almost all of the 200 rescued passengers, was conveyed back to Glasgow from Cloughey and took the next boat to New Zealand.

Rev. Thomas Burns: Among the first party of settlers for Otago to set sail from Scotland in 1848 was the person recruited as the first minister of the Otago Scots colony and the Dunedin Knox church. He was the Rev. Thomas Burns – a nephew of the Scots poet Robert Burns! A gener-

ation later, in what was described in the *Otago Daily Times* of 1882 as the defeat of 'Scotch Prejudice', opposition to instrumental music (and the exclusive use of Psalms) in the

Dunedin church was finally overcome, and permission was granted by the Dunedin Presbytery for the introduction of an organ in the Knox Church. The newspaper observed that it was *"only fit and proper that a congregation like that of Knox Church should conform to the manners of the place and time, and have its 'kist o' whussles' as well as Episcopalians, Methodists, or Baptists."*

Cloughey Presbyterians to the Rescue: When the *Wild Deer* ran onto the North Rock, two miles off Cloughey Bay, at 11.00 pm in a fierce storm, the first small boat to attempt to reach it was from the Coastguard Station, then a terrace of Coastguard Houses located on the shore near Cloughey Presbyterian Church. It was hopelessly inadequate to deal with such a monumental task as the rescue of

200 people. Indeed, only six months later, as a direct result of the shipwreck, a decision was taken to build a Lifeboat House and slipway right beside the church. The Cloughey Lifeboat House was opened in 1885.

The undoubted physical heroes on that night in January 1883 were the nearby Portavogie fishermen who shuttled to and from the North Rock in their shore-beached fishing boats. They had to repeatedly row the 4-mile round trip as sails were useless in the conditions. But, modestly, the fishermen themselves claimed the real 'heroes' of the night were the Presbyterian minister and his wife. The Rev. Alexander and Mrs Whitley not only raised the fishermen from their homes – mustered the operation – but also provided food and organised accommodation for the 200 souls brought ashore.

The manse and neighbouring cottages were able to take in some family groups, but this was inadequate, so the Rev. Whitley opened the church, lit the boiler and organised straw bedding for all the pews to serve as berths. Mrs Whitley and the womenfolk then organised enough food for the morning to feed all those that hadn't been housed in local cottages. As the next morning was a Sunday, virtually all the rescued passengers attended the 'Sabbath Meeting' in a hastily brushed-out Cloughey Presbyterian church, and a unique and emotional service was conducted by Alexander Whitley.

Rev. Alexander and Mrs Cecelia Whitley, "Heroes of the Rescue": The banner of Portavogie Jubilee Flute Band c.1910 celebrated the couple a generation after the event. (Photo: courtesy of Stephen R McCormick).

On Cloughey Shore

Tha wun whup't throu tha riggin rapes,
"Tha Wild Deer sails theday."
Tae New aZeelan, doon tha Clyde.
New lives a wheen wull hae.

Twa hunner sowls, as monie draims
In echteen-echtie three,
Tha Scotch Free Kirk's Dunedin toon,
Whaur truth micht set thaim free?

Tha hale Otago Province bocht,
Tha Free Kirk pass'd tha laa,
Fur thoosans haed aareadie gan
New life fur yin an aa.

But fisher-fowk on Cloughey Shore,
Knowed naethin o thair plan.
Whan fog on thon ruch wunter's nicht
Cum doon on sea an lan.

Tha mair a dizzen times afore,
Tha Wild Deer daen tha trip,
But noo tha tar-breeks loast thair wye,
An aff course they daed slip.

Tha Wild Deer ris an fell on roaks,
Twa mile frae Cloughey Stran,
Whaur Coastguaird Hoose, an Meetin Hoose,
Thegither, baith daed stan.

A figgerheid, tha Wild Deer haed,
Frae wood, a goddess hoak't.
Diana, goddess o tha hunt,
Scraich'd heich abane tha roaks.

A rocket flare, tha Coastguairds saa,
Abane tha Noarth Roaks flaff'd.
Tha Cloughey 'lifeboat' then set oot
Strang men, but hairts aye saft.

Tha ship wus stuck ticht on tha reef.
Her mast wus brok in twa.
Tha scraichs o weemin an o weans,
Wud brak yer hairt anaa.

Sae monie fowk that needit saved,
Sae smaa wus thair wee boat.
Tha only guid thing wus tha roak,
That kep tha ship afloat.

Tha lifeboat wusnae fit its lane,
Tha men caa'd, "dinnae greet."
"We maun noo get oor fishin pincks,
An Portavogie fleet."

Sae bak the' rowed tae Cloughey Shore,
An saa tha manse wus lit.
Tha dorr wus apen, doon tha pad,
A man stud at its fit.

"Twa hunnèr souls, or mair, tae save?"
Sez Rev'rent Whitley, "Jump!"
"We'll rise tha fowk, an man tha boats,
Frae here tae Buttèrlump."

Sae aa tha fishin boats an men
Pit oot tae sea thon nicht.
An weemin bakeit breid on peats
Fresh lit by greeshach bricht.

On Cloughey Shore, tha passengers,
A trickle, noo a flood,
Guidwives tuk hame, wi saut-wat tears,
As monie as they cud.

Tha manse wus fu, an iverie hoose,
Ay, richt tha shore alang,
Whan Mr Whitley brocht tha key,
Thon Meetin-Hoose wus thrang.

Cairt-loads o strae, a fairmer brocht,
Fur beddin in tha pews.
Tha boiler lit, in dead o nicht,
A geth'rin point fur news.

'Ma' Whitley gethert claes, an wat
Wairm tay fur thaim in need;
Tha manse rin oot, but roon aboot,
Tha neibors helped hir feed.

Amang tha Scotch, a passenger,
Frae Ballymena toon,
Wha fell an brok his leg thon time,
Tha mast cum creshin doon.

A dizzen lasses frae Bilfast,
Vere Foster'd lairnt tae coont.
Some sware the'd ne'er set sail again,
Fur fear o gettin droont.

In moarnin licht, tha fowks cum oot.
Maist didnae sleep ava.
They gethert at tha Meetin-Hoose,
Fur news o yin an aa.

Weel-fed an wattert, wairm an dry
Some cled in giftit blanket,
Alang wi hosts, redd up tha kirk,
An sayed, "Tha Loard be thankit".

Tha Meetin-Hoose, it cudnae houl,
Tha fowks that gethert thair,
Tae render thenks whan tae tha Loard,
'Da' Whitley made his prayer.

In twarthie days, tha passengers
Wur hame tae stairt agane.
That nane wus loast, wus nae man's boast,
But doon tae Him abane.

A sennicht gan, tha shore wus lown
Tha ship oot on tha roak,
Wus noo brok up, an some wi greed,
Amang its wreck daed hoak.

Otago's 'gowld-rush' wus a curse,
Its blessins tae corrup'.
On Cloughey Shore, in proof o that,
A figgerheid waash'd up.

Diana goddess o tha hunt,
Hir wudden image dumb,
In Talbotstoon wus lang syne seen
Tha Wild Deer's pagan stump.

Philip Robinson

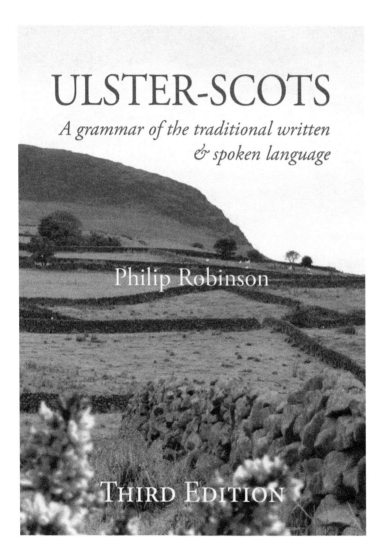

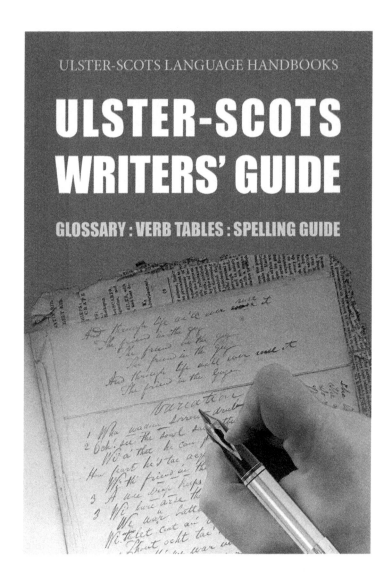

Tha Caves o Nerja

Mairble-airchit tebernickles
O dairkness. Naw,
In dairkness, ay,
(An ayewyes)
Tae five billie lumps
O lads wi tillie lamps
In year o '59
Raidin,
Expectin
Unnèrgrun
Fun
Nae empie towmb
But in new licht
Recreation's hoovin wame
Expectin.

Years wi'oot nummer, wattèrin
Yirth-siftit tears, pittèr-pattèrin
Frae Adam Yin

By Adam Twa, aa
Frae Abane
Tae noo an museum heids
An een tuk steps, an lectric lichts, an daen a dig, an
Fun
Stane-age hairts haed wrocht lang syne
In oker rid an or'nge
Paintit fish.

Day-trippèrs, chuff-chuff, dang-dang
Aff tae see
Doon pads an steps tha recoard o
Whut nae tongue cud tell
In airtfu scrolls
Hingin
Frae spricklie gothick roof
Bak-lit
Wi rid an or'nge lichts
A Tolkein sicht

An frae tha wheeshet echa-chaummer flair
Wat glintin tonsils
O stallickmites
Hoove an clim, an glancin

Echa thair brithers cries
Abane.

Thon Tony Gowdy ketched it weel
In Bercelona pile
In spires
Wi coupit creel
O stallicktites
An ither growein foarms
O Halie natur
Abane tha grun
Oot
In tha licht.

Whan Nerja trippers lee, an lichts gan oot
Wat trippin tears
O aa creatioun
Faa on, an on, an on,
In deein pains, intae its empie towmb
Or birthin pains, intae its hoovin wame
O recreation.

Philip Robinson

ON THONNER KNOWE

On Thonner Knowe

(Tune: Since Christ my Soul from sin set free)

A weel hae mind, whan A wus wee,
That richt fae wrang, wus plain tae see;
Then whiles doon on, ma hunckert knee,
A pray'd, Oh Loard, hae mind o me.
> *On thonner knowe, wha cud he be?*
> *That fur ma sins, he be'd tae dee.*
> *Oh Three in Yin, an yin o three,*
> *Thon middle Yin, He dee'd fur me.*

Yinst hairth an hame, wus aa A knowed,
Tae men o micht, then ootbye showed,
Sae thochts o pride, an doot wur sowed
An in ma heid, jist growed an growed.
> *On thonner knowe, wha cud he be?*
> *That fur ma sins, he be'd tae dee.*
> *Oh Three in Yin, an yin o three,*
> *Thon middle Yin, He dee'd fur me.*

But yin bricht day, tha wecht o sin,
Wus taen frae me, an left behin.
Fur Jesus tuk it on tha chin;
Sae hoo cud A, no follae him?
> *On thonner knowe, wha cud he be?*
> *That fur ma sins, he be'd tae dee.*
> *Oh Three in Yin, an yin o three,*
> *Thon middle Yin, He dee'd fur me.*

On thon dairk knowe, o Calvarie,
Jist like a wean, A cum tae Thee.
Cursed then wi sin, but noo set free,
Loard tak ma life, tha hale o me.
> *On thonner knowe, wha cud he be?*
> *That fur ma sins, he be'd tae dee.*
> *Oh Three in Yin, an yin o three,*
> *Thon middle Yin, He dee'd fur me.*

Philip Robinson

Tha Onyx Stane

Wisdom, mair precious nor tha Onyx stane
Thocht waefu Job, whan aa frae him wus taen.
An sae thocht Dauvit's prince, whan axt atween
Tha twa tae wale, afore tae him tha croon
                    An baith wus gien.

Ocht meesure't precious in tha thochts o man,
Aa enless vanitie, sung Salaman.
Tha buriet gowl deep hidlins unnèrgrun
In ither thochts, mair heich, lang intendit
                    Yit tae be fun.

Aa Job haed needit, lang syne wus plantit
Yit wisdom on mair heich grun then bideit
Fur whar wus he, axt God, whan tha deep foonds
O yirth wus layed, an Wisdom, Gowl an Onyx
                    Wus set fur croons.

Philip Robinson

Tha Blak Weeda Wabster

Forenenst tha burns o Babylon
Nae hairtsome sangs cud soond
Fur hairts knowed weel that thraldom's chains
Haed feet an thrapples boond

Thon Oul Man creepie-craalie thing
Wi belly on tha grun
Syne thocht yinst mair he'd flee abane
An up stye heichts he clum

Thon Unyvarsal Spidèr-Man
A warl-wide wab haes spun
Wi baa's o stickie-lickie threed
Whar aa can sing an thrum.

"Cum-aa-ye merrie hairts o Doon
It's apen an it's free
Tae sing yer ain sangs, 'mang yer freens –
But sangs o Zion, lee."

Whut's naw tae like, or love, or grue?
Aa yis cud want is here.
Untae yer chairge o power rins oot
An Wabster maks a steer.

Philip Robinson

Sarah M'Cready's Monkey

[Editor's note: Patrick Bell of Ballywalter is the father of a well-known Ards family of talented musicians, singers and song-writers, that sometimes perform and record as the group known as "Family Folk". This song, which Patrick wrote himself and set to one of his own tunes, is a true story and the source of great amusement locally. In fact, in Ullans 9 & 10 (2004), William Cromie published his own prose version of his stories about "M'Craidy's Monkey", and he related it in Ulster-Scots: "…Tha monkey wus soon a common sicht roon tha country. Ivrywhaur that tha twa brithers went tha monkey wus wae them, sittin on their shoothers if they were walking, or on tha hannelbars o tha bike if they were ridin them. They wudda sometimes tuk it on tha bus whun they were gan tae Newton. Whun they wur working in tha fiels it wudda been tied wae a length o rape tae a bush, an it played aboot tha dyke wae tha oul dug". Here we have another set of humorous anecdotes of 'M'Cready's Monkey' not only with a different slant, but also in a different medium: a 'traditional' ballad.]

Sarah M'Cready's Monkey

Noo Alec M'Cracken sailed o'er the wide ocean
An went tae the Amazon forests o rain.
An while he wus oot there, he tuk a great notion
Tae bring a wee monkey back hame again.

Weel the monkey objectit tae bein' deported,
An displayed its reluctance tae leave its big trees.
It scolded, an snortit, protestit, cavorted,
An made it weel knowed that it wusnae best pleased.

Noo Sarah M'Cready leeved in Ballywalter
In a raa o wee hooses, no far fae the shore.
An Alec decided tae gie her the monkey
For weans, she had nane, an she wantit yin sore.

Still thranin at its unceremonious disruption
The monkey wi crabbit intention did glare.
An Sarah, for fear o a troubled adoption
Tethered fast tae the leg o a chair.

Her husband (caa'd Rabbie) enjoyed the odd Guinness,
An the monkey wus gien some, an it liked it as well.
But M'Cracken "laced" the porter wi sweet cherry brandy,
An a scunnert drunk monkey can cause merry hell.

Wi strenthenin fury it broke free its tether,
Bit Sarah's left leg, an run oot the front door,
An wi skills that it learnt in Brazilian weather
Run up John Bell's spoutin, the roof tae explore.

The spairks frae its tae-nails wur flashin an dancing
As over the Bangor blue slates it did skid,
An screamin wi anger, an tae fast advancing
Wi drunken abandon, it made for the ridge.

Noo even a monkey that's weel used wi climbin
Can mak a misjudgement whenever it's fu'.
An blin tae the danger, crashed intae a chimley,
An sprachled an panicked, an fell doon the flue.

James Henry Dunbar wus a hairmless oul crater
Wha sut by his fireside, readin for fun.
He lached, as he lukked at the "Dandy" an "Beano"
Oblivious tae whut wus descendin the lum.

In a clood o black reek, wi the soot an spairks fleein
The monkey appeared wi a blid-curdlin' scream.
Its eyes they reflected the flames o the fire,
An its white teeth wi threatnin menace did gleam.

"It's the divil!" yelled James Henry jumpin in terror,
The monkey's mad eyes burnin intae his soul.
An the monkey it danced the best jig in all Ireland,
Whaniver its feet landed on the hot coal.

Wi the speed o a man half his age, oul James Henry
Bolted oot the front door, an run up the Main Street.
For whaniver Beelzebub comes doon your chimley
It's easy the advancin' years tae defeat.

Sae he made for the shore for his life needed savin,
An he niver lucked back as the harder he ran,
An he lucked at the Galloway coast as a haven,
An he even thocht o the far Isle o Man.

But the monkey had run in the ither direction,
As feart as James Henry, an goin' as quick.
An the monkey was puzzled, befuddled, an muddled
An bewildered at bein' behel' as oul Nick!

But at last it wus captured an gien some black coffee
An it lay for a day, for its heid was that sair.
An in future it stuck tae the Guinness when drinkin'
Cherry Brandy, it swore, it was "niver, nae mair."

James Henry for his pairt sut back fae the fire
Whan readin the "Dandy" an "Beano" for fun.
But niver again would he sit free an aisy,
Wi yin ee suspiciously watchin the lum.

Sae Alec M'Cracken went back ower the ocean,
An oul Ballywalter was queeit again.
An Sarah M'Cready wi mitherly dotin',
She raired thon wee monkey, like a wean o her ain!

Ding Doon tha Mairch Dikes

an Ulster-Scots translation of Bakhtiyar Vahabzade by Steve Dornan

We aye big mairch dikes
for tae houl oor ain,
an say: "aathin on this side
belangs tae me".
Ach, ding doon tha dikes
an cowp the waas o tha bawns
for tae keek at ither airts,
ootby, oot thonder.
Folks' dwams wull no thole
bein cleeked in kists;
na, they gie tha braes a dander
an lowp tha sheuchs
fae screich o day tae dailygaun.
As lang as folk hae een in their heids
they'll glower at thon
braid horizon.

An mind ye dinnae redd oot
tha geelgowans an buckies;
dinnae sned tha leevin roots.
Nature wull no thole
bein cleeked in kists:
it maun hae mair nor
rig an fur.
An aye mind that we're no
bits on a chakkers board,
on sindert squares o tha yin colour.
For dwams aye
jink an jook aff
ayont tha braidest horizons.
Aye, ding doon tha mairch dikes
an cowp tha waas o the bawns,
for tae keek at ither airts,
ootby, oot thonder.

Steve Dornan's *Jaa Banes*

(The Ulster-Scots Academy Press, 2020)

reviewed by Alan Millar

PUBLISHED in early December of 2020, Steve Dornan's 60-page ground-breaking volume of poems and prose *Tha Jaa Banes, An Ulster-Scots Collection*, has added a much-needed and welcomed injection of creative energy into the contemporary Ulster-Scots literary scene, challenging commonly held assumptions about the language in the process.

The striking gothic of the front cover image sets the tone for what's to come, as throughout the poems and occasional prose pieces are composed in rich Ulster-Scots language.

Steve's literary creation 'Ronnie Steenson', a quintessential aule school Ulster-Scots bard, is comprehensively formed, using multiple devices to build up the layers of his character. He is immediately recognisable, and you could place him among any of the irascible aule characters still to be found, yearning for a bygone world but with a nuanced eye on the present.

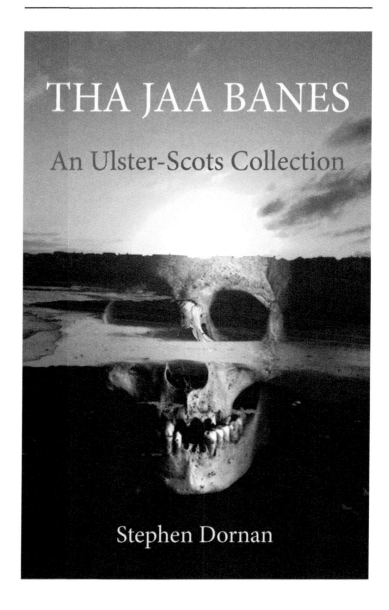

Our character is introduced by an unnamed narrator, who, using a device common in Scots literature, discovers a corpus of writings in a Lambeg Drum, at Ronnie's wake. Now, *'fash yer heid wi (a) dictionary'*, for Ronnie's Ulster-Scots is as dense as anything used in the tradition, going back to William Starrat in the 1750s.

Steve, like us all, has to come to terms with the depletion of the language in traditional areas. Unlike his invention, Ronnie, his own rich language is presumably partially book- learned. Correctly, he embraces this fully and without apology, though ironically Ronnie, with little need of a dictionary, would probably have cast a condescending eye on his maker, revelling in his own 'native-spoken' marginalized, ill-understood, *'screed o blethers.'*

The collection is divided into two parts, with a second smaller corpus of work emerging later. This tantalizes the reader with tha possibility of even more poems, lost thanks to the nastiness of a second character, Ronnie's long-estranged daughter, living in England.

The prose introductions to the initial poems cover similar ground to the poems, but it is through these that Ronnie's reasoning and the source of his inspiration, old stories deep rooted in the community, are conveyed.

Powerfully symbolic, 'The Gellick' (earwig), written in the classic Scottish 'Habbie' verse form, serves as a statement of intent, embracing Ulster-Scots in the 'subject treating' tradition of Thomson's 'To a Hedgehog' or Orr's 'Tea' and is a fine addition to this tradition.

'McBane's Skull' and the title poem 'Tha Jaa Banes' are without doubt the most magically inspired poems in the Ulster-Scots tradition that I have ever read. Both are a smorgasbord of Ulster-Scots and, though a reasonable 'aule han' at the *leid* by this stage, I occasionally needed a dictionary.

Throughout, a clacking cacophony of words and syllables run rough cut and smooth. Lines from 'Tha Jaa Banes', read as follows:

> 'Like clatters o coorse folk crackin
> 'Yarnin, bletherin. slabbrin, colloguin,
> 'Yappin, yowchin, clackin'

Ronnie's *'dailygaun'* wanderings take him through a world of traditional Ulster-Scots set props: sheughs, loanens, whun bushes, toonlans, plantins, queelrod waas etc. Ronnie *cowps* into a sheugh, and reflections as an Ulster Protestant 'Planter' are provoked as he spots a thistle while lying in on his back on top of the soon-to-be unearthed Jaa Banes (no more spoilers).

His insights are old school, harsh but insightful. They are *'houl yer ain'*, not rights based, but profound: Ulster and Scotland, *'sib and sinnert'*, close as family but separated.

Other times Ronnie's antics in 'Tha Jaa Banes' seem to be about celebrating the use of the delicious vocabulary rather than having a deeper purpose. And why not!

'Belfast, Efter Good Friday', is a broody, alienated matt eyeing the busy gloss of the city, with Ronnie's character considerably built upon in this poem. 'Tha Twalfth Day' is a sketch of a traditional Twelfth with traditional historical narratives described more than updated or revised.

Here, as elsewhere in the collection, words and phrases echo purposefully of Orr, Fenton, and others, nods to the tradition of which he is in the latest generation. The fight stanzas are reminiscent of the fight in Thomson's 'Simmer Fair', written in the same Scottish 'Christis Kirk on the Green' stanza.

Introduced by the unnamed narrator as before, Ronnie's second collection is less powerful than the first, though strong interest is maintained. In each of the sonnets to L.L. MacCassey, Ronnie offers different perspectives on this historical figure, the engineer who first mooted the bridge to Scotland. He is an archetypal Victorian-era Ulster Protestant hero for many of Ronnie's vintage.

I was somewhat confused as to how the 'Translations fae Nagorno-Karabahk' actually related to that part of the world, though the poems themselves were interesting, with some fine moments. I loved the lines in 'Tae be Yersel':

> *"Ye think me thran an wee*
> *A bawn-heided planter?*
> *But A hae made sheuchs o oceans*
> *An bigged heivens abin drumlins."*

This grand-scale vision is also captured in the course of the 'Tha Bovedy Meteorite', hurtling through space and down the page in the opening poem of this section.

Ronnie is probably too thran and reclusive to do all the *'dingin doon'* suggested in the final poem, 'Ding Doon tha Mairch Dykes', but typically he is well fitted to urge others. This returns me to the fact that the author is Steve Dornan, not Ronnie Steenson.

One has the feeling that, as well as providing a vehicle for Steve to immerse himself in traditional Ulster-Scots language and culture, Ronnie has also helped him keep difficult and complex subjects at arm's length. But there is no doubt that this is an important addition to the corpus of Scots writing in Ulster.

Steve has left himself well placed to build on this literary achievement in a further collection, something I would eagerly anticipate.

Tha De'il, tha Grogan an tha Hare Wutch

Ulster-Scots are a solid, God-fearing, no-nonsense lot with no time to waste on superstition or tales of the powers of darkness.

No? Well, on further consideration, perhaps you're right. Folklore and folk-belief may not be nearly as widespread as once they were. They seem to belong in many families to two or three generations ago; and tales of encounters with the supernatural are usually told at one or two removes from the person involved in the encounter. Stories of the fairies were common in the past, and many a Presbyterian elder has hesitated to cut down a fairy thorn in the middle of his field; the devil was omnipresent, if variously, in religion and folk-belief and is portrayed in a multitude of ways; and beliefs about witches were not easily dismissed in the community. The three poems reproduced here were written in the first decade of the twentieth century yet, light-hearted as they mostly are, they draw on community folk-beliefs from the writers' wider experience.

In his book *Pat McCarty*, in 1903, John Stevenson re-marks that 'stories of the fairies are without end and they are not all old stories'. He continues: 'In a county {i.e. Antrim} which includes manufacturing Belfast and fashionable Portrush it is to be expected that the little people will be unequally distributed.' It is unlikely too, he says, that they will be found 'in the neighbourhood of spinning mills and shipbuilding yards ... but in the quiet country of the east and north-east, on the edges of bog and moorland, on the mountains and in the glens ... the fairies are as numerous as ever.'[1] The fairies, he records, are said to 'weave at night on cottage looms, and use the smiths' forge. They are "the good people" but if you have offended them ... they will have their revenge.'[2]

Indeed, the moorland mentioned by Stevenson becomes identified in tradition as a favourite locus for encounters with the powers of darkness. Stevenson's own poem "De'il's Tricks" opens with the line, 'If on some lonely moor by night...' Wesley Hutchinson in his discussion of 'marginal spaces' in Ulster-Scots tradition also identifies moorland, or the moss, as being associated with the supernatural and the occult, citing both Stevenson's poem and also Burns's "Address to the Deil" in which Burns 'sees the moss as a space where people are most likely to encounter manifestations from the other world that place them in mortal danger.' Burns's best known tale of an encounter with the supernatural, "Tam o' Shanter", where 'a drunk man who has to cross the moss at night and … who meets with supernatural phenomena' is echoed in Ulster-Scots literature by Robert Huddleston's tale of "Doddery Willowaim."[3]

Burns's descriptions of the Devil had an interesting effect on the Presbyterian community's 'diabolology' according to "Cowan Harper".[4] In his autobiographical account of his County Antrim childhood at the end of the nineteenth century, Harper argues in fact that, unfortunately, Burns's 'homely anthropomorphic description' of the Devil 'weakened the De'il's powers in religious matters by extracting some of his terrors… Without losing altogether his pronounced Satanic features our Scottish Devil was such that we sometimes addressed him, à la Burns, with homely familiarity, even exposing his quasi-human weaknesses and apparent injustices.'[5]

The 'Grogan' is the Irish equivalent of the Scottish 'Brownie' and is associated with the fairies. Just as the fairies helped around houses and workshops, Grogans were said to help around farms, especially at harvest, with threshing and other tasks. However, they were said to take offence if offered recompense or reward for their work. One person interviewed in the middle of the nineteenth century reported: 'The Grogans used to give great help to them they took a fancy to. They are little men, about two feet high or so, stout built, broad-shouldered, and as strong as any twelve men. One of them gev great help to my grandfather, time after time, at the harvest... But the Grogan gev the most help in the winter at the thrashin'; many a sack of oats he thrashed for my grandfather...'[6]

In his discussion of witches, Stevenson records how they are often believed to be seen in the form of a cat or a hare. 'A hare or a cat is seen, is suspected of being a witch, is shot with a silver piece, and the witch in human form is afterwards found to be wounded in a part of the body corresponding to that in which [the] cat or hare suffered.'[7] This is broadly the story in Robinson's "Betty Rogers and the Hare" except that the old lady avoids assault or death at the hands of the young lads, if only at the last minute, when one of them spots the hare under a bush. It may be that Robinson had heard the story or had witnessed something similar in his youth. Certainly, in the last stanza of the poem, Robinson invites the reader to contemplate the

injusticc of the death suffered by many women simply on
the suspicion of witchcraft.

John Erskine

DE'IL'S TRICKS

If on some lonely moor by night
Ye're dand'rin' by the moonbeam's light,
Miles far awa' frae haunts o' men,
The hour a lang way after ten,
A dark man by your side ye fin',
And on the heather taps behin'
Ye hear the whuskin o' a tail
(Your heart fast thumpin' like a flail),
I dinna need to you to tell,
Ye're wi' the muckle de'il himsel'.

If while ye're cairtin' hame the peat,
The horse is lifted aff his feet,
The cairt is coup'd, and a' the load
Gaes hoppin', jiggin', doon the road, —
A turf across your lug comes whack,
Anither tak's ye on the back,

Anither bangs ye on the croon,
Or what ye sit on, lower doon,
Ye'll ken by tricks like these and squeals
Ye're in the hands o' sarvin' deils.

If, seein' no one anywhere,
Ye hear lood laughter in the air;
The chairs jump up, the tables turn,
The yellow butter leaves the churn,
Big, bleezin' fires are on the hill,
Your money changes in the till,
And meal and praties disappear
Withoot a mortial human near,
My worthy frien', you bet your sark
The mischief is the fairies' wark.

If at the time the sun gaes doon
Ye hear a weary, mournfu' soon',
Now sabbin' low, now swellin' high,
A lang, wild, wailin' deathly cry
That dies awa' wi' Och onee,
God save ye, frien', it's the banshee.
Frae de'il, the muckle one, himsel',
Frae a' the sarvint imps as well,

Frac fairy sma' and lone banshee,
May you and I presarvit be.

John Stevenson, *Pat M'Carty, farmer, of Antrim: his rhymes
with a setting*. London: Arnold, 1903.

JAMIE SMITH AND THE GROGAN

Auld Jamie wuz a wee-bit man,
    A hunchback, that wuz patent,
His heicht some three feet an' a span —
    Or mair, if he wur straighten'd.

Auld Jamie kerrit aye a rod,
    Gaed quate-like, nivir speakin',
In iviry hole he liked tae prod
    For eggs an' rebbits sneakin'.

In yon auld Wee-park's broken wa'
    He shoved his rod wanst lichtly,
But cudna' get it back a'va —
    Seemed somethin' held it tichtly!

He tuk baith han's, an' set his neck,
    His heel sunk in the soddie —
The hauld let go! an' Jim fell back
    Three times right ower the body!

Whan he got up, an' rub't his nase,
    He heerd a sniggerin' neer him,
Aboon him caw'd a flock o' cra's,
    He thocht they meened to jeer him!

But whan he keekit ower the wa',
    A wee man, broon an' hairy,
Wuz runnin', sniggerin', like tae fa',
    Nae bigger than a fairy!

Quo' Jim: "The Grogan's tricks I ken!
    His hauld I gart him slacken,
He thinks himsel' a match for men,
    But fegs ! he's sair mistakkin'."

. . . .

Folks mak' their bogies, gods, an' deils
    In likeness o' themsels!
A man jeest sees an' hears an' feels
    What in his ain min' dwells.

W. C. Robinson, *Antrim idylls, and other poems*. Belfast: Mullan, 1907.

BETTY ROGERS, OR THE HARE WITCH

Auld Betty Rogers, bent an' lame,
    An' white like snow, though spry,
Lang herded beasts an' sheep an' game
    On lonely Cairn-a-nigh.

Six lads an' me, wi' grues a-piece,
    Were huntin' wanst a hare,
Weel kent for whiteness o' its fleece,
    Amang the heather there.

An' when the dogs were close an' thick,
    An' catchin' at its fud,
It squealt, an' limpt, an' "blinkt" them quick —
    It sunk as in the mud!

Thus vanisht, near to Betty's cot,
    The hare we thought to clutch!
The dogs an' lads that follow'd hot
    All swore it was a wutch!

An' sure anuf, beyont the wa',
    Amang hir gerden kail,
Ould Betty, hirplin', soon we sa',
    A' pantin', like to wail!

Wi' rage on hir we made a rush;
  "Hould on, my boys!" George cried,
When crulged below a heather bush
  The blinkin' hare he spied!

. . . .

Had George no seen the hare in time,
  We'd squelcht poor Betty's breath!
An' mony a yin, as void o' crime,
  For "wutch" was done tae death!

W. C. Robinson, *Antrim idylls, and other poems.* Belfast: Mullan, 1907.

Notes

1. John Stevenson, *Pat McCarty, farmer, of Antrim: his rhymes with a setting* (London Edward Arnold 1903) p. 158.

2. Stevenson, *Pat McCarty*, p.159.

3. Wesley Hutchinson, *Tracing the Ulster-Scots imagination* (Belfast: Ulster University, 2018) pp. 352-353.

4. The pen-name of Rev. Prof. Dr Samuel Angus, 1881-1943.

5. Cowan Harper, *The auld sinner* (Sydney: Angus & Robertson, 1938) p. 65.

6. 'Fairy annals of Ulster. No. 2,' *Ulster Journal of Archaeology*, vol. 7, 1859, p. 133.

7. Stevenson, *Pat McCarty*, p. 160.

The Burning Bush

Owreset frae the Inglis o Norman Nicholson

Whan Moses, in tha wasteness thinkin, funn
Tha whun-busch jeggin up frae oot het grun,
An seed tha brenches on a suddent bricht,
Tha crunklin yella flourish giein licht,

He reenged his ken an his imaginin
Fer some guid thocht or aisy raisonin
An turnt tae quit, an then tae bide, an knawed
Fu weel amid tha birnin busch his God.

A've seen masel tha breer alowe like pait,
Tha luive at birns, tha flesch at's aye complait,
An affen A hae turnt an lat it be,
Jalousin, "Parabil – it's Prophecie."

Yit jeggy tungs like Jhone tha Beptist cry:
"Tae houl this parabil bes nae ootwye.
God's no tae be mansweirt; this tenet's trow:
Tha busch bes aye a busch, an lowe's aye lowe."

John Erskine

The Lord's Prayer

A rendering in verse by James VI & I of the Lord's Prayer, containing elements of both Scots and English; or as Hugh Porter might describe it: 'Which is nor Scotch nor English either / But part o baith mix'd up thegither.'

The lordis prayer

Ô michtie father that in heauin remainis
thy noble name be sanctifeit aluayes
thy kingdome come, in earth thy will & rainis
euen as in heauinnis mot be obeyed with prayse
& giue us lorde oure dayly bread & foode
forgiuing us all oure trespaßis aye
as ue forgiue ilk other in lyke moode
~~preserue us from temtat~~
lorde in temptation leade us not ue praye
but us from harme euill deliver ever moire
for thyne is Kingdome ue do all record
allmichtie pouer & euerlasting gloire
for nou & aye ~~thus ue end~~ so mot it be ô lorde.

finis.

Transcribed from BL, MS Royal 18 B.xvi, f.44 as reproduced in David Crystal, Evolving English: one language, many voices: an illustrated history of the English language (British Library, 2010) p. 125.

John Erskine

The Dully Men of Ballywalter

Dully Men bringing dulse ashore

Along the coast of Co. Down there are several fishing villages where local inhabitants make a living from fishing for herring, mackerel, cod and shellfish, mainly prawns and crabs. The fishermen of Ballywalter, however, are unique in that their main occupation in the summertime is harvesting dulse. This is an edible seaweed that can be found in abundance growing on the rocks and kelp beds just off the coast of the village and is gathered at low tide when it can easily be reached. It was locally known as "dullys".

In late spring the men begin to prepare their boats and equipment in readiness for the start of the season. Firstly, the boats: these were mainly 14 ft. clinker-built boats that had been beached on a grass embankment above the shoreline during the winter months. A fire would be lit on the beach and a large iron pot with a block of pitch in it was placed on the fire. When this melted it was brushed onto the bottom of the boat, inside and out. Also, the upper part might get painted.

As these were rowing boats, the oars would be got ready. Firstly, two pegs, locally called thurl pins, would be fitted on the top side of the boat, a little bit apart with just enough room to allow the oars to move freely between them. Where the oars sat, a piece of leather would be tacked round them. This would be obtained from a local farmer, usually a piece of worn harness or scrap leather from a shoemaker in the village.

While this work was being carried out, there was one other very important task to do. The wet dulse would be spread out to dry on the shingle beach, known as the dully beach. This was an area of shingle about ten feet wide that extended from below the parish church to an area known as The Point. Members of the fishermen's families would go there with rakes and graips to clear away the debris that had washed onto it during the winter storms.

As this area was used mainly by four families – Dunbar, Eccles, Blair and Murphy – markers were set up allocating each family a stretch of the beach, usually a stone on the shore or a post on the bank above the beach.

With all the preparations made, it was time to row out to the rocks and kelp beds to find an area where the dulse was in plentiful supply. As the dulse could only be got at when the tide had ebbed well out, for this reason it was important to reach these areas about an hour or so before the tide was at full ebb. This would give the men nearly two hours to gather the dulse before the tide turned and was flowing in.

When they reached the kelp beds, the men would roll up their sleeves and then kneel down at the bow of the boat, reaching down into the water and cupping a hand round the stem of kelp. These were called 'tangles' which comes from the Norse word thang, meaning seaweed. The dulse attached itself to and grew on the stem. The men would pull the dulse off the stem and throw it behind them into the boat. This process would continue until the boat was filled or the incoming tide made the task too difficult.

It was time now to row back to the beach to spread the dulse on the shingle. The incoming tide assisted the rowing of the boat to the beach; once there the wet dulse was pushed into a sack and with their oilskin coats on they carried the dulse to the beach where it would be spread out. Sometimes other members of the family would be there to speed up this process. With this done, the boat would be rowed back to the harbour to be moored.

The men would then return home to change their wet clothes and have something to eat. They would later return to the beach to shake the dulse to speed up the drying. This time they took with them their only means of taking the dulse home, a four wheeler. This was a wooden cart with the wheels from an old pram attached. The front wheels swivelled to enable it to be steered.

The dried dulse was put in sacks called bales and taken home on the four wheeler where it was put into a shed or outhouse near the house. It was emptied onto the floor, so that it could be tossed over two or three times a day to allow the air to pass through it and prevent it from sticking together. This process continued until it was time to have it taken to Sawers in Belfast at the end of the week, when it was put back into the sacks and then weighed and labelled. It was then collected by the N.I.R.T.B. (Northern Ireland transport board) usually driven by Pat McKeown or Nat Carson, to be taken to Sawers where payment for the product would be made up individually for the respective owners.

After going by bus to Belfast to receive payment, they started on their way home. A sort of tradition some of the men had was to break their journey in Newtownards, where they went into Tate's pub in the square for what they called a couple of bottles of stout, and then to Morrison's the butchers for some of their renowned sausages. Then it was off home with money for the family and a well-earned rest before starting the process all over again on Monday.

In later years some of the boat owners used small outboard motors to propel their boats. Sadly this whole occupation has fallen out of use, as dulse no longer grows as much as it used to on the kelp beds. Whether this is due to global warming, pollution, or some other reason, no-one yet knows.

It is said that dulse has been harvested and consumed for over a thousand years, with early records of use in Scotland, among Christian monks. Today, the health benefits of consuming dulse in moderate quantities are being rediscovered, and it is recognised as a rich source of iodine and potassium as well as being beneficial for the reduction of inflammation. These are just a few of the claims that are made for it. Our forebears knew a thing or two.

Willie Cromie

A Case o Mistaen Identitie

It wus tha yeir twuntie an foartie-five. Gary Forgysin haed cum hame tae Ulstèr furtae leuk eftèr his seek mither, haein bocht hissel oot o tha ermy. His wark wi tha ermy wus whut tha offysers caa'ed 'sensitive', sae he wusnae leukkin tae be owre kenspeckle – in ither wurds he daednae waant tae stïck oot lek a sair thoom.

He kent tha oul sayin, 'Jyne tha ermy an see tha warl' – aye, he'd saa tha warl aa richt. Tha warst o't, but, wus 'at he wusnae aa that weel acquent wi tha wye o thïngs in Ulstèr itsel, fur tha sojers didnae hae tha leesure tae gae oanline fur newins frae hame.

Tha furst wheen o weeks bak in tha femlie hame in Aist Bilfawst, whun Gary wus leukkin pairt-time wark, he wus dumfoonèrt at tha little wark thar wus tae be haed. He cud aisie get a joab in yin o tha vegan burger places 'at wur aa tha go fur tha fowk 'at thocht the' wur 'on trend'. Thon wudnae dae ava, but, wi tha oors he wud hae tae pit in. Gin he fun an advert fur oniethin wi dacent pye, the' wud be leukkin a bodie 'at cud taak Airisch, an Gary cudnae dae't ava.

Gary gien it some thocht, an cudnae jouk tha notion 'at aa tha wye he cud airn a bït siller wud be tae set up oan his ain accoont. The mair he haed a pension frae tha ermy, he kent leukkin eftèr his mither wud tak a richt reuchness. Tha auld fowk mindit whan thar wus a 'National Health Service' 'at the' daednae hae tae pye fur – thae days wus lang gane, but.

Sae Gary gaed oanline furtae fyn a bodie trokin in motors 'at wudnae stïck tha erm in, pyed him a veesit an wi a feck o his pension he bocht a motor he cud rin as a texi. Mebbe he cud dae wi'oot haein tae git a private hire leeshins – naebodie wus makkin shuir thae rules wus follaed nooadays oniewye. He cud aisie advertyse hissel wi'oot haein tae lat fowk ken he'd bin a sojer. An he cud fit tha oors in roon leukkin eftèr his mither. He wusnae haein yin o thae thïngs 'at tracked ye, but. He'd jist hae tae uise his native wut an airt hissel tha wye he'd bin uised wi in tha ermy.

Tha wee texi consarn wus daein aa richt, an yin nicht he gat a hire wi a young fella 'at waantit tae gae ower tae Wast Bilfawst furtae see his lassie. He turnt oot tae be a richt fella an wus guid crack. He telt Gary him an tha wee cuttie haed rin agane ither in tha toon, ur whut wus left o't wi tha shaps aa gaein oanline, an haed clïcked. Up tae thenoo, but, the'd haed tae sen ither wee bïts o wittins oanline, fur tha lad, 'at the' caa'ed Erchie, wus hairt feart o his mither an faither fynin oot he wus rinnin wi a lassie frae Wast Bilfawst. He gien Gary a wee daud paiper wi tha lassie's address.

Gary skellied at tha scrievin. It micht hae bin haurd eneuch tae mak oot in Ing'lisch – this wusnae in Ing'lisch, but. 'Wud this be aa ye hae?' axed Gary. 'Och, ay,' sayed Erchie. 'Jist gae throu tha toon an oot tha tither side. It cannae be aa that teuch tae fyn'. Gary didnae waant tae lat oan he haednae tha new SDI, nivver mine tha oul-farrant GPS. Sae the' stairtit oot.

It wus aisie eneuch tae stairt wi. The' driv up whut Gary mindit as Kessel Raa – noo thar wus a sign up sayin 'sráid an Chaisleáin'. Erchie insensed him intil whut haed cum aboot in Bilfawst in tha twuntie yeir ur sae Gary haed 'bin awa'. Bak in tha fore-enn o tha twunties, tha cooncil haed brocht in a laa tae gie jist 15 oot o ivvery hunnèr bodies leevin in ilka raa in Bilfawst tha richt tae pit in fur a leid forbye Ing'lisch in tha sign at tha enn o tha raa. Oot o thon, a wheen o thoosan raas wus gien Airisch signs forbye tha Ing'lisch. Tha resydentèrs cud pit in fur Ulstèr-Scotch insteid, sae thar wus a wee clattèr o raas in thon leid – no monie, but.

'Ah weel,' thocht Gary, 'thon's no sae bad – tha Ing'lisch

marra o't wull be thar yit'. Hooanivver, tha fordèr up tha gate the' gaed, tha mair Gary's hairt whammelt doon intil his buits. Thar wusnae onie Ing'lisch ava. Eftèr, whanivver tha daeins o thon nicht wus ower, Gary fun oot 'at no lang eftèr tha signs gaed up wi tha twa leids tha resydentèrs ayther pentit ower tha Ing'lisch ur the' sneddit thon pairt o tha sign aff wi yin o tha unco shairp lectric bluetuith grindèrs 'at wus cummin in frae China. The'd nae last ava – the' wurnae dear, but.

This wus jist tha stairt o a lang nicht's rinnin roon Wast Bilfawst ettlin at kennin whar the' wur, wi Airisch signs alane tae airt thaim. The' wur up yin raa an doon anither. Thar wus naebodie aboot tha place furtae speir thair roadin, an Gary wus cannie aboot lattin tha resydentèrs ken thar wus twa uncos in thair airt oniehoo. Ivvery noo an agane, Gary stapped tha motor inunnèr a licht furtae hae anither leuk at tha wee daud o paiper whaur Erchie haed writ doon whut the' cried tha raa whaur tha lassie leeved. He cud mak naethin o't ava.

Twa oors ur sae intil aa this, tha motor wus jist aboot tae rin oot o chairge. A wheen o yeirs bak, tha govermin haed bin fasht aboot warlwide hettin, an haed brocht in laas furtae gar fowk hae motors 'at rin oan battèries. Whanivver thar wus ower monie o thaim takkin lowe and forbye thar wus a waant o tha cobalt an aa thae ither kyns o stuff tae mak tha battèries, tha motor makkers haed taen tent an pit siller intil bettèr technologie. Gary's motor wus yin o tha aulder yins, but, an thar wus naethin fur it but tae leuk a chairger 'at wus warkin.

Yin chairger haed bin wracked, anither wusnae warkin richt, a thurd wusnae takkin tha kyn o caird Gary haed. Tha twa o thaim wur aboot giein up whan the' cum oan a chairger in a supermairket station 'at wus yin o tha newer yins 'at wud gie a fu chairge in hauf an oor, an behoul ye it wus warkin! Sae it wus bak oan tha gate agane!

Aboot foartie mïnits eftèr, the' wur climmin a stye brae. Bae this, the wur oan a gate wi a sign 'at sayed 'bóthar an lóiste úir'. Gary thocht til hissel, 'Aye richt – bother's tha wurd!'. On a suddent, Erchie guldèrt, 'Stap! stap! Kermel sent her photie tae me wi l-mail, stannin afore thon biggin ower tha gate. A ken it weel! Thon wee raa doon tha side maun be tha raa whaur she leeves!'

Sae Gary turnt doon tha raa, an bae this jist tha yin hoose in tha raa haed a licht oan. Erchie lowped oot o tha motor an chapped tha dorr. Eftèr a mïnit tha dorr wus harlt apen an a muckle great man as braid as he wus lang wus stannin oan tha dorr-stane. 'Wha'dye want?' he guldert. Puir Erchie ganshed, 'Wud… wud… Kermel be in?' 'Av coorse she's in – at one in the mornin she's in her bed, same as aal dacent gerls.' Thristin a nieve lek a fitbaa unnèr Erchie's neb he gowlt, 'An ye shud go home to your own bed and don't come back!' Wi that he clashed tha dorr tae, lea'in Erchie stannin.

Bak in tha motor, wi tha licht frae tha hoose an tha raa forbye, tha twa trevellers haed anither leuk at tha wee daud o paiper wi whut tha raa wus caa'ed writ doon, alang wi tha lettèrin oan tha sign at tha enn o tha raa. Tha twa o thaim haed this lettèrin: شارع المستوطنين

Erchie sayed, 'Wud thon be Airisch?' Wi a shake o tha heid, Gary haed tae awn he didnae hae onie idea. It wus a dreich traik hame. Tha hale nicht haed pit him in mine o tha storie o Romeo an Juliet – it leukked lek Erchie an Kermel wusnae meant tae be. It taen Gary a wheen o days an a bït spierin roon neibors in Aist Bilfawst afore he gat tae tha bottom o whut the' caa'ed tha raa she leeved in.

Tha 'Belfast Area Plan' pit thegither in tha fore-enn o tha twunties, leukkin aheid til 2035, haed pit forrit tha govermin's lippent figgers fur 66 thoosan mair resydentèrs fur Bilfawst. In tha enn, thar wus aboot 72 thoosan cum intil tha citie, tha maist o thaim frae tha Mïddle Aist – no

Aist Bilfawst, mine ye. Seein tha citie cooncil haed made tha cheynge tae tha laa furtae alloo anither leid oan tha raa signs, aa tha incummin fowk threapit tae hae tha same thïng daen fur thair leid. Sae Kermel's raa haed gat an Arabic naem. Nae wunner the' gat loast!

Anne Smyth

Professor Robert J Gregg (1912 – 1998)

The following is the text of a speech made by the Ulster-Scots Language Society's Chairman at Larne Museum on Thursday 20th June 2019, at the unveiling of a plaque commemorating Professor Gregg, an eminent native of Larne. It is couched in simple terms because of the varying levels of interest in, and knowledge of, Ulster-Scots among those present.

Anne Smyth

Introduction

Thank you for the invitation to take part in this event. Larne and District Folklore Society's journal, *The Corran*, did a lot to cultivate interest in Ulster dialect over many years, and John Clifford, who wrote poems like 'Mounthill Fair' in dialect, was of course a stalwart of this very museum.

Professor Robert Gregg, to his delight, became Honorary President of the Ulster-Scots Language Society when it was formed in 1992.

But it was as Editorial Assistant on the Ulster Folk and Transport Museum's *Concise Ulster Dictionary*, starting in

1990, that I became aware of the importance of Professor Gregg's work to the academic study of Ulster-Scots. He was an Editorial Consultant on the four-person Editorial Committee that directed our methodology and gave the dictionary a firm educational basis. Importantly, he copied and posted to us, from Canada, his own meticulously hand-written dictionary slips.

I'd like to look at a few aspects of the Gregg story, and see what they have to say to us today.

(1) Gregg's linguistic distinction

Professor Gregg's gift for languages is seen in his command of French, German, Spanish, Latin and Russian. His forward-looking teaching abilities are evident from the fact that he set up a language laboratory at University of British Columbia, the first in any Canadian university. However, it was Ulster-Scots that was his lifelong passion.

Robert Gregg's hugely important Ph.D thesis, entitled 'The Boundaries of the Scotch-Irish Dialects in Ulster', was based on years of painstaking research. It has given us the only proper mapping of the Uster-Scots speech areas that has ever been done.

In contrast to much uninformed opinion on the subject of the Ulster-Scots language, Professor Gregg's views command respect because they are based on sound academic research. Some of them were expressed in 1994, in a private letter to the late Dr Ian Adamson, in these terms:

> 'To put it bluntly, I find it incredible that any specialist in language and dialect (I am one myself and have hundreds of others among my colleagues and acquaintances) – that any such specialists could regard Ulster-Scots as a regional variant of English! Impossible! … I feel these people are writing nonsense about Ulster-Scots not being a language but a dialect of *English!* Ridiculous!'

During the later stages of work on the dictionary, Robert Gregg chose to go through his own written papers changing references to 'Scots Irish' in his texts to 'Ulster-Scots' (hyphenated), as a more appropriate title for the language.

Another significant contribution to the study of the language was Robert Gregg's orthography, which he devised along with Brendan Adams, the first Curator of Language at the Ulster Folk Museum. The modern revival movement has wrestled with the problem of how to show Ulster-Scots pronunciation in writing, most recently in the work of the Spelling Standards Committee, set up by the Ulster-Scots

Academy Implementation Group. Gregg and Adams proposed some interesting solutions. Anyone who would like to see some of Gregg's transcriptions can find them on www. ulsterscotsacademy.com, in issues 2, 3 and 4 of the Ulster-Scots Language Society's journal, *Ullans*.

It was perhaps Robert Gregg's inborn ability as an educator that gave him the vision for the creation of an Ulster-Scots Academy. In response, the Ulster-Scots Language Society founded its sister organisation of that name in 1993. Although it achieved a lot, and continues to do so, it was not until 2005 that the Ulster-Scots Academy Implementation Group, established by the Westminster government, commenced fulfilling its remit to 'progress, without delay, the [specified] ongoing language development programmes of the Ulster-Scots Language Society'. So for the first time these programmes were properly resourced.

This work continued successfully for about 18 months, housed, appropriately, in the old Regent House School building where Professor Gregg had taught at the beginning of his teaching career in 1934. However, in late 2007, the Department abruptly terminated the work of the USAIG and Robert Gregg's vision for a fully-fledged Ulster-Scots Academy sadly remains unfulfilled.

(2) Gregg's character – generosity and persistence

It is a mark of the man that, despite daunting health problems that would have discouraged anyone less determined,
Professor Gregg continued to photocopy his material and
forward it to the Museum, to augment the resources from
which the *Concise Ulster Dictionary* drew. Our experience
confirms that of students and researchers who have praised
his generosity in making available the fruits of his research
to others in the field, in contrast to so many in the academic world today, where funding pressures have encouraged a
much less open attitude.

In the modern world, it is difficult to persuade people to give commitment to any cooperative project. I don't
know about the Ulster History Circle – maybe you have an
abundance of committed workers – but most organisations
struggle to find folk who will help 'keep the show on the
road'. In 1951, however, Professor Gregg joined a number of
other distinguished linguists in the collection of Ulster ver-
nacular speech by Belfast Naturalists' Field Club, using the
questionnaires devised for the Linguistic Survey of Scotland.
One was Professor Angus McIntosh, who became the main
supervisor for Gregg's Ph.D thesis. Another was Brendan

Adams, with whom Gregg worked to devise an orthography for Ulster-Scots. This is another instance of Robert Gregg's generosity with his time and learning.

As the dialect specialist at the Museum, I found this generosity reflected in Professor Gregg's family, as we received the donation of his Ulster-Scots language papers and library from his widow, Millicent. Later, we were greatly assisted by his daughter, Margaret Gilley, in our arrangements for the launch of the Museum's memorial volume entitled *The Academic Study of Ulster-Scots: Essays for and by Robert J. Gregg*, which I co-edited with Professor Michael Montgomery and Dr Philip Robinson. This is a milestone publication, which we trust will have a beneficial effect in changing public attitudes to the status of Ulster-Scots as a language worthy of study.

The other character trait of Robert Gregg that I wish to mention is persistence – persistence exemplified by his continuing engagement with the dictionary project despite serious health problems. This was clear right from the start of his academic career. There is evidence that the academic establishment at Queen's approached the choice of subject for his M.A. dissertation with something less than enthusiasm. Indeed, there is the suggestion that this attitude may have contributed to his decision to emigrate to Canada, where he found a more receptive environment.

Professor Gregg was in no way deterred from his pursuit of the study of his beloved Ulster-Scots language. He returned to Northern Ireland many times to progress his research, including for a protracted visit in 1960 – 61 to complete the fieldwork for his Ph.D thesis, culminating three decades of informal observation and collection. Today's Ulster-Scots speaking community is greatly indebted to him for his pioneering work in establishing the study of the Ulster-Scots language as an academic discipline.

(3) Robert Gregg's identification with his subject-matter

Anyone who studies dialect will know that people become so used to hearing their own dialect spoken that they often fail to notice that it's dialect at all. For the young Robert Gregg, however, his natural ear for speech differences quickly registered the contrast between the urban modified English he heard around him at Larne Grammar School and the dense Ulster-Scots language of his grandparents and other residents of Gleno, where he visited at holiday times. So, unusually, he began collecting linguistic material as a teenager. By 1930 he was compiling a notebook, and that was the start of a lifelong interest, at first eagerly discussed with his mother and brother in particular.

Add to this the fact that Professor Gregg remained an Ulsterman to the core, with a highly-developed sense of place, regardless of his long residence in Canada. And of course there were his long visits 'home' to pursue fieldwork. These factors combined to ensure that he was no 'ivory-tower academic', so stuffed full of learning and achievement that he could not identify with the speakers of his subject language. Furthermore, he seems never to have been tempted to explore the rarified terrain of sociolinguistics, whose proponents tend to spend a lot of time speculating about the ulterior motives of those seeking to promote and protect Ulster-Scots without actually asking them why they do it. So Gregg would never have found it dfficult to elicit information from his informants – a *thran* bunch who clam up if they encounter hostility. And he was left free to make a detailed study of the language *for its own sake.*

The texts chosen by Robert Gregg to test his new orthography were always local and often humorous. However, it was always beyond question that he was laughing *with* his fellow Ulster-Scots and not *at* them. Today, the Ulster-Scots language is frequently a matter of derision, directed at the language by those whose real knowledge of it can be minimal. To his great credit, Professor Gregg never contributed in any way to such attitudes, for all his learning, but on the contrary he pursued a lifelong mission to enhance the academic status of the language.

I'd like to give one short example of the type of exchange that Robert Gregg transcribed, showing the reader how the words should be pronounced. This is part of Glenoe's oral tradition, and to my knowledge never appeared in print until it was published in *Ullans 2:*

Thrawen Oul Jone an his Nebby Nybour

N.N.:   Thaat's a graan' moarnin, Jone.

Jone: Weel, ye hae yer share o't!

N.N.:   Did ye git aw thon rain yäsTerday, Jone?

Jone: Aa got whut fell on me.

N.N.:   Irr ye taakin thon wee coo tae the fair, Jone?

Jone: Aa'm shoor she's no fur taakin me!

N.N.:   Irr ye fur sellin' her, Jone?

Jone: Aa'm shoor Aa'm no fur bestowin 'er.

N.N.:   Is thaat yer sän ye hae wae ye, Jone?

Jone: Weel, Aa raired 'im onnywey.

N.N.:   Ye'r gey an' shoart the day, Jone.

Jone: Aa'm jist as laang as ävver Aa wuz!

N.N.:   Äar ye awaw, Jone?

Jone: Aa'm nether a waw nur a stane dyke!

Conclusion

We have looked at a number of aspects of the immense contribution of Robert Gregg to the study of Ulster-Scots. What might we be able to draw out from them?

Firstly, there is his linguistic distinction. Two main points arise: the lack of educational provision for Ulster-Scots, particularly in tertiary education. If we are ever to build upon Robert Gregg's legacy, Ulster-Scots will have to be studied as a language, and it will have to have a presence as of right in the education system. Then, too, Robert Gregg is an excellent example of the academic rigour and commitment that should be required of any academic specialists produced by the system.

Secondly, his generosity and persistence. All too often Ulster-Scots enthusiasts treat the language as if it were their own personal preserve. It has to be treated as a subject that we would love to see the world embrace, and that is capable of being learned. And we have to be persistent in promoting it.

Thirdly, his identification with the language. Ever since Ulster-Scots became the language of the ordinary people, it has been treated with derision, not least by those who think themselves learned. Robert Gregg's love of and commitment towards Ulster-Scots is the gold standard.

In Memoriam

James Fenton
(1931 – 2021)

James Fenton, who passed away on the 2nd of February, 2021, was President of the Ulster-Scots Language Society. He first made contact with the Society in the person of Dr Philip Robinson, when he visited the Ulster Folk and Transport Museum to talk about his researches into the Ulster-Scots of North and East Antrim. This had been ongoing since Jim began his survey of the speech of a carefully-documented range of speakers from the 1930s onwards, centred on his own home area of Ballinaloob but expanding its reach to Bushmills and Ballycastle on the north coast and Larne and Whitehead on the east, through the rural heartland of Antrim.

At that time, in the early 1990s, Dr Robinson managed what became the Concise Ulster Dictionary project, edited by Dr Caroline McAfee and funded by the Department of Education Northern Ireland. As Jim discussed his findings, Caroline and Philip were immediately enthusiastic about the potential benefit to the Ulster-Scots language from making the fruits of this research accessible to the public.

The Ulster-Scots Language Society had just been formed in 1992, arising out of the efforts of a group of activists who met in John McIntyre's kitchen, driven by the urgency of reversing the erosion of the language in face of the onward march of 'standard' English. Right from the start, there was an emphasis on projects that would display the authentic language while also showing its credentials as a subject with a good pedigree, worthy of study in its own right.

It was obvious that James Fenton's research was admirably suited to this objective. Caroline McAfee shared the attitude of her mentor, the great Jack Aitken, whose work on Scots language remains unparalleled, in making their knowledge available to other researchers, and she readily

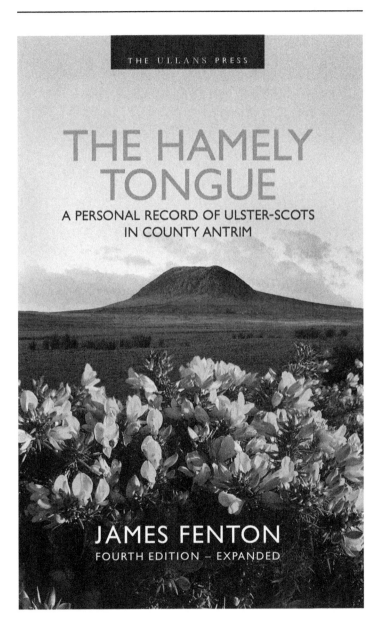

THE ULLANS PRESS

THE HAMELY TONGUE

A PERSONAL RECORD OF ULSTER-SCOTS IN COUNTY ANTRIM

JAMES FENTON

FOURTH EDITION – EXPANDED

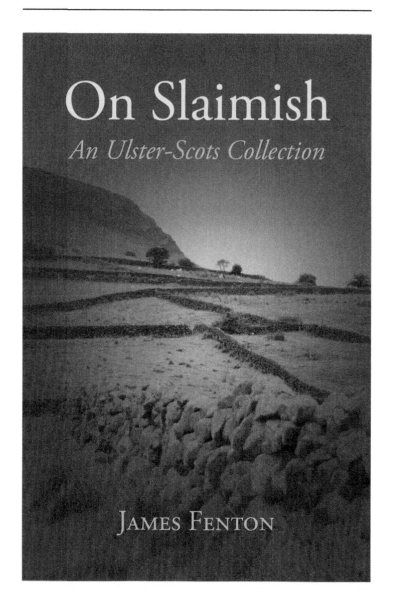

agreed to assist James Fenton with proper organisation of the text and the origins of words where available.

Jim, however, pointed out a difficulty with all this: 'Who will publish it?' he said. 'We will', responded Philip Robinson. 'Who's "we"?' Jim queried. 'The Ulster-Scots Language Society', said Philip. So began the close collaboration between James Fenton and the USLS that culminated in his election to the position of Honorary President of the Society.

The new society was totally dependent on subscriptions and donations to stay operational, but occasionally it succeeded in obtaining a grant from government bodies for individual publications. These were the days before 'publish on demand' became a possibility, but if any project was worthy of support, this one certainly was.

In the following months, James Fenton became a frequent visitor to the Museum, clutching sheaves of paper, while the editorial assistant (the current USLS Chairman) pounded away at the keyboard, reading from Jim's immaculately handwritten script, and Caroline McAfee gave gentle and informative guidance on etymologies. Computers were not to his taste at all. Jim was meticulous about accuracy and authenticity, and everything was checked and double-checked. However, he was always the gentleman, unassuming and wonderful to work with.

The culmination of this painstaking work was the publication in 1995 of the first edition of *The Hamely Tongue: A Personal Record of Ulster-Scots in County Antrim*. Several editions later, this remains, together with Philip Robinson's companion Ulster-Scots grammar, an Ullans Press best seller. It is unique among dictionaries in that it puts the words and phrases in context, bringing the language to life.

Academics and other researchers who do not identify with the Ulster-Scots community find that when they attempt to elicit Ulster-Scots speech from their subjects, the interviewees instantly revert to English. This is how the urban myth of 'no native speakers' came about. The genius of Jim's work was that he was of that community and so there were no barriers. Although Jim went on to study at Queen's and became a teacher and school principal in Belfast, his sense of connection to the place where he was brought up never left him. Collection of the words and phrases of his North Antrim countrymen and women was an all-consuming, lifelong interest.

Nor was his knowledge of Ulster-Scots only theoretical. He had included short pieces of his own Ulster-Scots writing in his dictionary text, and Philip was so impressed with these that he asked if Jim had written anything else. More bundles of paper arrived, and we realised that this was the work of the greatest Ulster-Scots poet of our generation. Jim's standing as a writer was such that he could rub shoulders with such greats as Seamus Heaney and Michael Longley.

Jim was a skilful writer of Ulster-Scots in both prose and poetry. His poetry was first published in our Society's journal, *Ullans*, but later his books, *Thonner an Thon* and *On Slaimish* (which also eventually featured in several BBC programmes), were published to acclaim that went far beyond the world of Ulster-Scots. It is totally natural and real, and redolent of ways of life that are passing away – the lade, the flow, the lint dam, and the innocent friendships of younger days. Hearing Jim read his poems was an experience no one could forget. The dense Ulster-Scots of his writings frequently confounded those unaccustomed to hearing or reading the language and was a counter argument to those that insisted Ulster-Scots was only a dialect.

Towards the end of his life, Jim's health deteriorated and he rarely left home. Unfortunately, during this time great distress was caused him by the publishing of a book called *The Other Tongues: An Introduction to Irish, Scots Gaelic and*

Scots in Ulster and Scotland. In brief, this book, published by 'Irish Pages', edited by Frank Ferguson and funded by various public bodies including the Ulster-Scots Agency, not only misrepresented the legal status of Ulster-Scots in its front matter but also featured Jim's signature poem 'On Slaimish' without permission (when it would have been easily obtained), complete with typographical errors and a 'glossary' (although Jim had made a point of never including glosses of the vocabulary in his writings) that was replete with egregious errors and serious blunders of comprehension, such that parts of the poem became meaningless.

The Society became involved because not only had the intellectual rights of the writers (both Jim Fenton and Philip Robinson) been ignored but so also had the reproduction rights that resided with Ullans Press, the original publisher. In a move that added insult to injury, Irish Pages sent a cheque for £100 to Jim (and the other two parties) as compensation for the wrong the publisher had perpetrated; but no-one involved had ever asked for money and the cheques were never cashed. Instead all three parties were only seeking an apology that was never forthcoming. The USLS takes very seriously its responsibility towards those who entrust it with reproducing their work, and it is distressing that in this instance it was unable to protect the rights of a poet whose like we shall never see again.

Jim's talent was hugely appreciated by his friends in the USLS. He will be remembered with enormous respect for his abilities, but for us in the Language Society also with deep affection.

> Belnaloob's whar A come frae,
> The hamely rit o maist A'll hae,
> Whun a' bes ower, tae fang'l wae;
> An aply fin
> The jag wuz gien as weel tae spae:
> A towl ye, sin.

Professor Michael Montgomery – a 'Mighty Warrior' for Ulster-Scots

Michael Bryant Montgomery (May 15, 1950 - July 24, 2019) was a Past President of the Ulster-Scots Language Society who was no passive bystander in the fight for survival and recognition of the language. In previous tributes to him the word 'courage' comes up time and again. He was pressed down by cruel physical impairments, yet never allowed himself to be defeated by them. In a tribute to Michael a couple of months after his death, a friend wrote 'We're all wimps compared to him', a comment with which we in the Language Society would concur.

Originally from Tennessee, Michael at length became a Professor Emeritus of the University of South Carolina. His interest in the culture of the parts of America settled by Ulster-Scots immigrants extended to Appalachian music, and at one point he sent the writer a CD of one recording that Michael was at pains to describe as totally authentic. It is still not entirely clear whether this was one of his many pranks, but suffice to say that it did not become an instant favourite in the recipient household.

Michael's first encounter with the Language Society occurred in the early 1990s, when he was just discovering his Ulster connections and came to the Ulster Folk and Transport Museum to speak to Philip Robinson about family history. His quest for his family's roots took him to Greyabbey, which he revisited faithfully on each annual visit until he became unable to make the journey. As his lovely niece Rachel said in her memorial to her uncle, 'His romantic heart cherished history and wanted to use his powers to fight to preserve it'.

At the time of Michael's first visit, Philip and his museum-based colleagues were in the early stages of work on the *Concise Ulster Dictionary*, and Michael followed this enterprise with a professional eye. On one occasion, he had received an invitation to Belfast Central Library to attend a launch event, and the writer, then the Editorial Assistant on CUD, was delegated to accompany Michael to the occasion.

She deposited him on the pavement right in front of the library and went to park the car, but on returning found that he had disappeared. This decidedly junior functionary on the CUD project stood confounded on the city centre street, experiencing a wave of panic at having mislaid this eminent academic. What could have happened to him? After some searching, Michael was located, happily availing of the food on offer at the launch and chatting easily to other attendees. It seemed that library staff had spotted him and escorted him through an entrance unknown to the public, to bypass the steps.

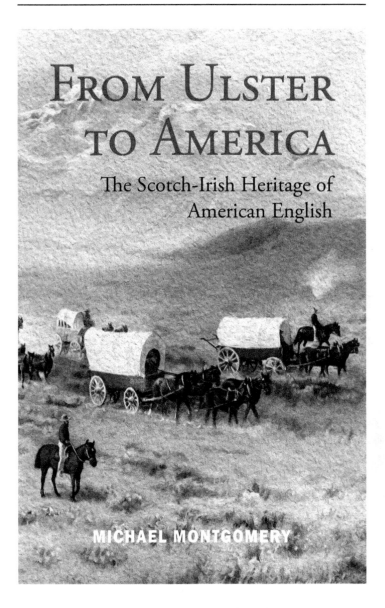

FROM ULSTER TO AMERICA

The Scotch-Irish Heritage of
American English

MICHAEL MONTGOMERY

DICTIONARY
of SMOKY
MOUNTAIN
English

Michael B. Montgomery

Joseph S. Hall

Michael was the Ulster-Scots Language Society's Honorary President until 2015, but he was never content to accept the plaudits of an honorary office rather than be an active protagonist for the Society and the language. His contribution took many forms: articles for previous issues of this journal (the first appearing in 1994 in the second issue), advocacy and interaction with Stormont departments, language planning, and particularly giving direction to our sister organisation, the Ulster-Scots Academy.

In regard to this last category, a prime example was 'An Academy established and the task begun: A report on work in progress'. This report, written in 2003, was published in two versions: Michael Montgomery, 'An Academy Established and the Task Begun', in *Ullans* 9/10 (2004), 102-11, and (based on this report), Anne Smyth and Michael Montgomery, 'The Ulster-Scots Academy' in John M Kirk and Dónall P. Ó Baoill (eds.), *Taking Stock in the Literature, Sociolinguistics and Legislation of Minority or Regional Languages in Northern Ireland, the Republic of Ireland, and Scotland* (Belfast Studies in Language, Culture and Politics 13), (Belfast, Queen's University Belfast, 2005), 60-64 (reprinted in *Review of Scottish Culture*, 17 (2004/05), 106-10).

When DCAL abruptly closed down the work of the

publicly-resourced Academy at Regent House, leaving its untrained functionary to rummage through and supposedly document the Ulster-Scots Language Society archives that had been deposited there on foot of a partnership agreement between the Society and the Academy, Michael went to Regent House to investigate the breach of the Society's rights and confront the person directly responsible. Even those of us who were Michael's allies in the battle for proper recognition and resourcing for Ulster-Scots had encountered his searching questions, delivered in that deep, powerful voice that left no room for obfuscation or prevarication in return.

While Michael could be formidable in the right cause, he was also extremely considerate in sharing his wide knowledge with others. Many have expressed gratitude for the generous scholarly support colleagues and those he mentored received from him.

Michael became one of the foremost authorities on the connection between Ulster-Scots and some varieties of speech found in American English. His researches resulted in several historical volumes and ultimately his major work, *The Dictionary of Smoky Mountain English*, published in 2004. On this side of the Atlantic, perhaps his best known book on these important links is *From Ulster to America: The*

Scotch-Irish Heritage of American English. He also assisted on *The Dictionary of American Regional English (DARE)*.

On a personal note, the writer benefited greatly from Michael's learned contribution to the highly influential work *The Academic Study of Ulster-Scots: Essays for and by Professor R J Gregg* (2006) which was co-edited with Michael and Dr Philip Robinson. A memorial volume to the great pioneer of the academic study of Ulster-Scots, Professor Robert Gregg, this was the result of several years of research, compilation and editing.

Because Professor Gregg had been particularly interested in the orthography of Ulster-Scots, that is, an accepted spelling system indicating pronunciation, it was necessary to purchase a software system that would replicate the necessary symbols. Although there was some similarity with the International Phonetic Alphabet, some symbols used by Gregg were different; but a system was chosen that we could adapt. This involved several keystrokes for a single letter, so progress was slow.

One of the health difficulties with which Michael struggled was poor eyesight, and there had been modifications to his PC to enable him to read the screen more easily. He did not have access to the software used by the other two editors. This meant that data sent electronically underwent unscheduled amendments en route. In these circumstances, the only remedy was to send portions of the text via fax. It is a measure of Michael's dedication to the task that he persevered and indeed was meticulous in checking what was sent to him.

His determination not to let his physical difficulties hold him back is also seen in his travels outside of the USA. Michael kept in close touch with his family and took great delight in watching the stages of development of his six nieces and nephews. This entailed a trip to West Germany to visit his sister, and also to Russia on the same occasion and later to act as best man at the wedding of his younger brother in 2000. Michael was plagued with problems in sleeping, and travelled with bulky extra equipment to improve on the comfort of unfamiliar bedding.

Another affliction with which Michael had to contend was poor hearing. Ultimately he had a cochlear implant, but this only slightly improved things. In telephone conversation, despite an adaptation of the handset to sharpen the sound, communication was slow and repetitious. Michael never reconciled himself to feeling that he was remote from the heart of the Ulster-Scots battle, and every now and again he would telephone one or other of his Language Society friends in what usually became an epic call. The record was achieved in a conversation with one member that lasted from 8.00 pm to one o'clock the following morning!

An outstanding facet of Michael's character was his enduring Christian faith. During his telephone calls, notwithstanding the hindrances to good communication, he always had a word of spiritual encouragement in the fray, and this is greatly missed since his passing. Although it is a comfort to know that now he is beyond all the pain and suffering he endured in life, our Society is very much the poorer for his loss. His is an example of unselfish commitment that is all too seldom encountered.

> Tha mair A waak throu daith's dairk glen,
> Yit A'll no fear ocht ïll:
> Fur thou art wi me an thy cruik
> An staff, gie comfort stïl.

Dr Ian Adamson OBE
(28 June 1944 – 9 January 2019)

Dr Ian Adamson was a founding member and first Chairman of the Ulster-Scots Language Society from its formation in 1992 onwards.

Born and raised in Conlig, Co. Down, Ian Adamson was well acquainted with Helen's Tower, which is where the Belfast Brigade of the 36th (Ulster) Division trained prior to being sent to England in May 1915 and from there on to France for the 'big push', which became known as the Battle of the Somme. In adult life, the Tower and what it represented were to become an object of intense interest for Ian Adamson.

Professionally, he was a medical doctor specialising in paediatrics. Perhaps out of an associated concern for the physical and mental welfare of young people, he became involved in the Farset Youth and Development Group. It was while he was on a trip to Europe in the late 1980s with youth groups from the Shankill and Falls, and Tallaght and Inchicore in Dublin, that he initiated a detour to the Ulster Memorial Tower, and from that point on he sought to increase awareness among the upcoming generation of the sacrifice of the fallen of the First World War.

In 1989 Dr Adamson became a founder of the Somme Association, serving as its first Chairman. He was at that time also pivotal in the drive to restore the Ulster Memorial Tower at Thiepval, France.

Ian Adamson was involved in politics as a representative of the Ulster Unionist Party, and held political office at local government and Stormont level. He retired from active politics in 2011.

Although he was active in a wide range of interests, today Dr Adamson is mainly remembered for his historical research on the Cruthin and their retreat from Ireland after the Battle of Moira. Because this narrative directly contradicts that of Irish nationalism, which proposes that the Celts (whose identity is itself controversial) are the original inhabitants of Ireland rather than one wave of invaders among several, the proposition occasioned much vehement controversy. However, Ian Adamson's objective in introducing this story to the public was the promotion of a common origin account that would bring the people of Northern Ireland together.

Ian Adamson's wit and gregarious nature won him a wide circle of friends and acquaintances, including such varied notables as Van Morrison and Cardinal O'Fee.

Dr Adamson claimed a faciity with a number of languages, including Ulster-Scots. Despite his interest in the language he was not a native speaker, although he did make a short scripted speech in Ulster-Scots in the Stormont Assembly in the early days of its existence.

After the Ulster-Scots Language Society was formed in 1992, the Ulster-Scots Academy was created as its sister organisation to cater for members with a more specialist interest in research and study. The Academy was the vision of Professor Robert J Gregg, the pioneer of the academic study of Ulster-Scots, who had emigrated to Canada, and Dr Adamson was one of those who visited him there to discuss how this could be established.

It is a cruel irony that when eventually the fully-resourced Academy was formed on the initiative of the Westminster government, after it had functioned effectively for about 18 months the individual appointed by the Department for Culture, Arts and Leisure to abort the project was in fact recommended to the department by Ian Adamson.

By 2008, which was the time of these events, Dr Adamson's interest in the work of the Language Society seemed to have waned, and on several occasions the Society tried to re-establish contact with him, initially with the intention to nominate him for an honorary position within the organisation. He did form an academy-type body which he entitled the Ullans Academy, but apart from a few annual prizegiving events at Stormont it does not seem to have been active in research or study in Ulster-Scots.

It is impossible to avoid being impressed at the enormous range of interests of Dr Ian Adamson. He was a true polymath, of a type that is rarely encountered in modern times. The Northern Ireland scene is the poorer for his passing.

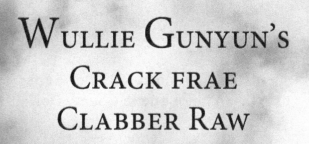

WULLIE GUNYUN'S
CRACK FRAE
CLABBER RAW

ROBERT LEE MOORE

Edited by Philip Robinson
& Anne Smyth

THE LEEVIN TONGUE

An historical record of Ulster-Scots as a living language in County Down

ROBERT LEE MOORE

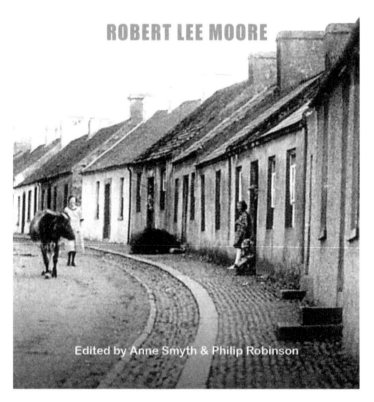

Edited by Anne Smyth & Philip Robinson

Printed in Great Britain
by Amazon

36516649R00079